Please Love Me Like I Love You

♥ My love for you will never age.
Find a heart on every page... ♥

Written by Kip Ullrich Fechner
Illustrated by Janis Ullrich Dillon

Published by Pet Kindness Press

Copyright © 2020 by Pet Kindness Press

All rights reserved. This book or any portion thereof
may not be reproduced or used in any manner whatsoever
without the express written permission of the publisher
except for the use of brief quotations in a book review.

Printed in the United States of America

First Printing, 2020

ISBN 978-1-7334215-0-8

Pet Kindness Press
1229 South Vandeventer Avenue
St. Louis, MO 63110
314.652. 9924

PetKindnessPress.com

This book is dedicated to our beloved dad, Dr. Ray Ullrich,
who taught us to respect and be kind to all animals, especially dogs.

Written with love for our grandchildren: Heidi, Margot, Samuel, and Mabel.

Special thanks to Angela Ponder, Graphic Designer, St. Louis, MO.

I am your dog.

Always be nice and ever so kind.

Pet me nicely and don't ever tug!

Please love me like I love you.

Don't pull my ears!

That hurts!

Oh, my!

Hearing your voice is special to me,
like a sweet lullaby.

Please love me like I love you.

Don't hit or grab my face...

that makes me sad!

Don't kick me!

I am not a ball.

Being rough won't do at all.

Please love me like I love you.

Make me happy
and always show that you care.

Please love me like I love you.

I am so happy to see you
and that's the reason why.

Please love me like I love you.

Don't jump on me when I am sleeping!

I get tired and need to rest.

We all need sleep to be our best.

Please love me like I love you.

Don't touch my food while I am eating!

It is my food and it upsets me so.

Please love me like I love you.

But that dog doesn't know you and might be afraid.

Always, always ask "May I pet your dog today?"

So follow all these dog rules
about being extra kind.

To bite you is the last thing
I will ever want on my mind.

I think I have covered
all I wanted to say.

Remember, yes remember,
a love between you and me is so special,
it will never go away.

You mean everything to me...
you really do!

Please love me like I love you.

www.ingramcontent.com/pod-product-compliance
Lightning Source LLC
Chambersburg PA
CBHW051355070526
44584CB00025B/3769